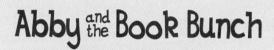

Abby and the Book Bunch

MOVIE MISHAPS

by Nancy K. Wallace

illustrated by Amanda Chronister

magic wagon

visit us at www.abdopublishing.com

For my husband, Dennie, and my original Book Bunch: Hanna, Derrick, & Dakota
—NW

Printed in the United States of America, North Mankato, Minnesota.
102012
012013
 This book contains at least 10% recycled materials.

Text by Nancy K. Wallace
Illustrations by Amanda Chronister
Edited by Stephanie Hedlund and Rochelle Baltzer
Layout and design by Neil Klinepier

Library of Congress Cataloging-in-Publication Data
Wallace, Nancy K.
  Movie mishaps / by Nancy K. Wallace ; illustrated by Amanda Chronister.
    p. cm. -- (Abby and the Book Bunch)
  Summary: Abby is having trouble coming up with a community helpers project since all the other children in her third grade class have taken all the good jobs and even her best friend is planning on doing something without her--but the public library beckons.
  ISBN 978-1-61641-914-1
1. Student volunteers in social service--Juvenile fiction. 2. Public libraries--Juvenile fiction. 3. Books and reading--Juvenile fiction. 4. Elementary schools--Juvenile fiction. 5. Volunteers--Juvenile fiction. 6. Community and school--Juvenile fiction. 7. Best friends--Juvenile fiction. [1. Voluntarism--Fiction. 2. Books and reading--Fiction. 3. Public libraries--Fiction. 4. Elementary schools--Fiction. 5. Schools--Fiction. 6. Best friends--Fiction. 7. Friendship--Fiction.] I. Chronister, Amanda, ill. II. Title.
PZ7.W158752Mov 2013
813.6--dc23
                                        2012027942

CONTENTS

Off to a Bad Start 4

Pet Projects 10

Nobody Wants Egg Salad! 17

Stormy Weather 22

Pancakes and Picture Books 28

The Perfect Job! 35

Surprising Mr. Kim 40

Story Time 46

Rubber Frogs and Cow Balloons 52

Lunch with a Vampire 60

Movie Magic 66

Technical Trouble 72

The Book Bunch! 77

Off to a Bad Start

"Wait for me!" Abby called. She raced down the steps of Perry Elementary School.

Abby's best friend, Sydney, stopped and turned around. Kids rushed past her to find their buses.

"I thought we were going to talk about our Community Helpers Project at recess," Abby said, zipping up beside her. "Where were you?"

A bright yellow leaf whisked across Sydney's sleek blonde hair and skittered off. Sydney turned her back to Abby. She looked up the street at the row of buses and cars.

"Katie and I walked down to the swings," she finally said.

"We can work on it this afternoon," Abby suggested. "Do you want to come over?"

"My mom is picking me up," Sydney said. She wobbled her front tooth with her finger. "I'm going to the dentist, remember?"

Abby made a face. "I forgot. Maybe tomorrow, then. You can sleep over. I already asked my mom."

Falling leaves suddenly rained down on the girls'

heads. They stuck in their hair and piled up on their book bags. "Hey!" Abby yelled, turning to see who was throwing them.

Dakota stood grinning behind them. His freckled cheeks were red.

"Oh, it's you." Abby giggled as she untangled a leaf from her brown curls. "You're so lucky, Dakota! You already know what you are doing for your project. Sydney and I don't have one yet."

Sydney shifted from one foot to the other. She didn't look at Abby as she said, "Abby, I do have a project. Mom asked if I could help at our church. Katie and I are going to visit Evergreen Nursing Home twice a week with Pastor Elizabeth."

Abby's lower lip stuck out. Tears stung her eyes. "Why didn't you tell me before, Sydney? I thought we were going to do a project together."

"I'm sorry," Sydney said, looking at the sidewalk. "Katie goes to my church.

My mom talked to her mom about the project without telling me."

A blue van pulled over to the curb. Sydney's mom waved at Abby and Dakota. "See you tomorrow!" Sydney said. "I'll ask about sleeping over."

"Best friends forever!" Abby called. But Sydney just waved. The van door slammed shut.

Abby kicked at the leaves by the curb as the van sped away. "What will I do for a project now?" she asked Dakota.

"I'm going to miss my bus!" Dakota yelled. He ran off, dragging his book bag behind him. The canvas scraped and bounced on the cement.

Abby stood alone. "Bye," she called. But Dakota didn't hear her. He was already climbing into the bus.

Abby turned to cross the street. She wished Sydney was walking home with her.

"Hi, Abby!" said Betty, the crossing guard. She had a big yellow button on her bright green crossing guard vest. It said "SMILE." Abby didn't feel like smiling.

"What's the matter, honey?" Betty asked, bending to look at Abby's face.

Abby shrugged. Her book bag bounced up and down on her back. "All the third graders have to be community helpers for a month," she said. "I don't know what to do."

"When's your project due, honey?" Betty asked.

"We have to tell our teacher where we will be working by Monday," Abby said.

Betty stood up and smiled. She

patted Abby's shoulder. "Then you have the whole weekend to come up with something. Don't you worry."

"I don't have any ideas!" Abby said.

"Ask your grandma," Betty suggested. "I'll bet she can help you think of something!"

Gram always had time to talk. She was staying with Abby for a few days while her parents were away. Maybe they could come up with a project together.

Abby gave Betty a big smile. "Thanks, Betty," she said. "See you tomorrow!"

Pet Projects

"Hi, sweetie!" Gram was waiting when Abby crossed the street. She gave Abby a hug. "Did you have a good day?"

Abby nodded. It had been a good day until she found out she and Sydney wouldn't be doing a project together.

"Mom said Sydney could sleep over tomorrow night," Abby said. "I asked Sydney today. Mom left money to order pizza."

"Pizza it is!" said Gram.

They walked down the block past the red brick public library. Mrs. Mackenzie, the children's librarian, was just getting out of her car. She had a huge bear puppet in her hand. Abby waved. "Hi, Mrs. Mackenzie!"

"Hi, Abby! Hi, Mrs. Simon!" Mrs. Mackenzie called back. She made the bear wave his paw at Abby. "I just came back from telling stories at the preschool. Are you coming to the library?"

Abby shook her head. "Not today. We're coming on Saturday."

Mrs. Mackenzie smiled. She waved the bear's paw again. "See you on Saturday, Abby!" she said in a deep, rumbling voice.

Abby laughed. She and Gram walked down the block to Abby's house. The maple trees that lined the street had turned bright red and yellow. Gram had been raking the front yard. One side of the yard was finished. Leaves still covered the other side.

"I can help you rake," Abby offered.

"Change your clothes first," said Gram. "I want to finish before the rain starts tonight."

Gram unlocked the door. Abby's golden retriever, Lucy, ran to greet her. Lucy pressed her cold, wet nose into Abby's hand. Her tail wagged her whole body back and forth.

"Hi, Lucy!" Abby said, patting her head.

Lucy ran into the yard. She snuffled along the ground under the bushes. She came back with a wet, dirty tennis ball.

"Wait, Lucy," Abby said. "Let me run up and change."

"I made sugar cookies," said Gram. "We can have one before we rake. I'll meet you in the kitchen."

Abby ran up to her bedroom. Lucy followed right behind her. Her doggie face was smiling. Abby took off her school clothes and found jeans and a sweatshirt. She raced Lucy down the stairs. Their feet clattered on the steps and the hall floor.

"You sound like a herd of elephants!" Gram said, laughing.

A plate of sugar cookies sat on the kitchen table. They had orange icing and sparkly sugar. Gram poured milk into two glasses. Lucy flopped down under the table.

"So, how was school today?" Gram asked.

"Okay," Abby answered. She broke off a piece of cookie and fed it to Lucy. "I think I need your help with something."

Gram sat down across from her. "I'll be glad to help," she said with a smile. "What do you need?"

"All of the third graders have to pick a project. Sydney and I were supposed to do it together. But now she's working with Katie. I don't know what to do," she said.

"What are some of the other kids doing?" Gram asked.

"Sydney and Katie are helping their pastor at the nursing home. Dakota is helping our teacher," Abby told her.

Gram laughed. "I'll bet everyone wanted to help Mr. Kim."

Abby nodded. Everyone liked Mr. Kim. "Yep, but Dakota thought of it first."

Gram took a bite of cookie. "Well, we'll just have to come up with something special. Think about the things you like to do. Maybe that will give you an idea."

"I like to play with Lucy," Abby said, stroking Lucy's head.

"Maybe you could help at the animal shelter," Gram suggested.

Abby smiled. "That's a good idea! Maybe I could walk the dogs!"

"Let's call right now," Gram said. She got out the phone book and put on her glasses. Her finger skimmed down the list of numbers. "Here it is: Lawrence

County Animal Shelter. Do you want me to call?"

Abby nodded. She didn't know anyone at the animal shelter. Having Gram call sounded like a good idea.

Gram dialed the number. When someone answered, she explained what Abby needed to do. "Oh," she said. "I see. Well, thank you anyway. Have a nice day!"

Abby smiled. Gram always told everyone to have a nice day.

Gram put the phone down. "Well, I guess some other kids had the same idea. They have four third graders who want to walk dogs. They don't need anyone else."

"Oh," Abby said in a small voice. "Mr. Kim only assigned this project yesterday. So many kids have already found places to volunteer. What if I can't find a project?"

Gram gave her a big smile. "Don't worry," she said. "We'll think of something!"

Nobody Wants Egg Salad!

At lunch on Friday, Katie ran ahead so she could sit with Sydney. Abby sat on the end of the bench. She opened her lunch box and pulled out her sandwich.

Dakota plopped down, too. "I'll trade you my egg salad for your turkey sandwich," he said.

Abby shook her head. "I like turkey sandwiches. Egg salad smells funny."

Dakota sniffed his sandwich. He made a face. "What do you have, Sydney?"

Sydney flipped her hair to one side. "Cold pizza," she said. "We had it last night for dinner."

Dakota's eyes were on Sydney's cheesy slice. "Want to trade?" he asked.

"No," Sydney answered. She took a big bite and looked at Dakota. She chewed very, very slowly. "Mmm, this is so good," she said after the last chew.

Dakota looked at Katie's lunch tray. "What about you, Katie?" he asked.

"Don't even ask," Katie replied.

Dakota rolled his eyes. He bit off the corner of his sandwich. "So what did you decide to do for your project?" he asked Abby.

"I'm still trying to think of something," Abby answered.

"You could read to the preschool class," Dakota suggested.

Katie smirked. "Morgan and Ethan are already doing that," she said, licking ketchup off her finger.

"How about cleaning up the park?" Dakota said. "I'll even drop off more trash for you to pick up."

"Robby, Noah, and Alexis signed up for that yesterday," Abby said, trying to smile. "Don't worry. Gram and I are going to think of something really special."

"Too bad," Katie said, munching on her hot lunch. "Sounds to me like all the really special jobs are taken. You're just out of luck, Abby."

"Wait and see," Abby answered. She hoped Katie wasn't right. What if all the special jobs were taken? What if there weren't any jobs left at all?

Friday afternoon went quickly. After lunch, they worked on fractions. Mr. Kim had paper pizzas and apple pies to cut into pieces.

Rain splashed against the windows. The wind howled. Twice the lights flickered. Then, they went out!

The room was really dark. Somebody screamed and the boys laughed. Dakota made spooky sounds and waved his fingers in Abby's face.

"Now, now," said Mr. Kim. "It's just a storm. Stay in your seats."

The lights came back on after a minute.

"I guess we'd better watch this movie while we can," Mr. Kim said. He pulled the blinds down and popped in a DVD. Soon, it was time to go home.

"You only have until Monday to choose a Community Helpers Project," Mr. Kim reminded them.

Abby slid down in her seat, hoping he wouldn't look at her.

"See me after school today if you haven't found a place to volunteer yet," Mr. Kim said.

But, Abby didn't stop to talk to Mr. Kim after school. *We have the whole weekend to think of something,* Abby thought. *Gram and I will think of the perfect place for me to volunteer.*

Stormy Weather

Gram picked Abby and Sydney up after school. Abby held her book bag over her head as she ran to the car. Wet leaves stuck all over the cement steps. Water ran in the gutters. The windshield wipers whisked back and forth faster and faster.

"What a nasty day!" said Gram. "This is quite a storm!"

Gram drove down the block. She pulled into their driveway. Then, she handed an umbrella and the key to Abby. "Run, run, run!" she said.

Abby and Sydney raced up the sidewalk. The girls splashed through the puddles as the rain pelted down. Sydney giggled as Abby fumbled with the key.

When the door swung open, Lucy was waiting.

"Hi, Lucy!" Sydney said, patting her.

Gram ran in behind them. Water ran off her coat and pooled on the floor. "I have snacks in the kitchen!" Gram said.

Abby and Sydney decided the first thing they wanted to do was make friendship bracelets. Abby got her new bead set from her room. She and Sydney worked at the kitchen table. They chose pink and purple beads to make the bracelets.

"Let's put them in this cup," Abby said. "If they roll off the table, Lucy will eat them!" Lucy wagged her tail and smiled.

Just then the lights went off. "Oh no!" Abby cried.

"Sit still," said Gram. "I'll get some flashlights." Gram's flashlight snapped on. She handed one to Abby and another to Sydney.

"I'll call the power company," said Gram. In a few minutes the phone rang. Gram answered it. "It's your mom, Sydney."

"Hi, Mom," said Sydney, taking the phone. "No, we're okay. We have flashlights." She looked at Gram. "Mom wants to know if you want her to come and get me."

"Don't go," Abby moaned.

"You stay right here," said Gram. "We have everything under control."

"The power is out all over town," Sydney said, when she hung up. "My dad is a fireman. He says a big tree blew over on one of the lines."

"No pizza!" Abby groaned. "What will we have for supper?"

"We can cook in the fireplace," said Gram. "It'll be fun! Would you girls get me some logs from the porch?"

The girls carried their flashlights down the hall. The lights bobbed along in front of them. They opened the door to the back porch. Rain clouds darkened the sky. The yard was covered with broken twigs and leaves. The afternoon looked like nighttime. The streets and houses were dark.

"It looks weird," said Sydney.

"Like a spooky movie," said Abby.

They each carried two logs into the living room.

When they got there, they found Gram had made a tent out of a blanket! It stretched from the top of the couch to the top of the recliner. Inside, she had put a lantern.

"We'll pretend we're camping!" she said.

Gram lit a fire. Abby and Sydney cooked hot dogs on long forks. Then, they roasted marshmallows for dessert.

"This is fun!" Sydney said. She licked marshmallow off her fingers. "It's better than pizza!"

"Can we sleep down here?" Abby asked.

"Why not?" said Gram.

"I'll get the sleeping bags out of the closet," Abby offered. She dragged them to the living room. Lucy chased the ties across the floor.

Abby and Sydney spread the sleeping bags out under the blanket tent. Gram brought pillows from upstairs. The tent looked cozy and warm. Lucy jumped on top of the sleeping bags. She lay down and put her head on the pillows.

"Lucy has the best spot," Sydney giggled.

Abby and Sydney finished their friendship bracelets. They played board games and made shadow pictures with the flashlight. They read all of Abby's library books out loud.

"It's a good thing we're going to the library tomorrow," Abby said. "I'm out of books!"

Sydney didn't answer. She was busy fluffing up her pillow and climbing into her sleeping bag.

Pancakes and Picture Books

Abby woke up when Gram peeked around the corner of their tent. "Who's hungry?" Gram asked. "I made pancakes!"

Lucy stretched and yawned. She sniffed the air and then followed the girls into the kitchen.

"The power is back on!" Sydney said in surprise.

"It came on in the middle of the night," said Gram. "You two were sound asleep."

Abby sat down at the table. "I can hardly wait to go to the library this morning," she said.

Sydney looked at the floor. "I can't go, Abby. Mom's picking me up at ten. Katie and I have to talk to the pastor about our project."

Abby put her fork down. She didn't look at Sydney. Abby swung her foot against the chair. *Tap! Tap! Tap!*

After a minute, Sydney said, "I'm sorry about the project, Abby. I really didn't know my mom was setting everything up."

Abby looked at her plate. "It's all right," she said.

Lucy put her head on Abby's knee and wagged her tail. Abby gave Lucy a piece of pancake.

"I'm really sorry," Sydney repeated. "I hope you find something really, really special."

"I will," Abby said. She let Lucy lick the sweet syrup from her finger. Her warm tongue tickled. "I know I will!"

After Sydney left, Gram and Abby walked to the library. Their neighbors were picking up branches in their yards. A chain saw roared at the house next door. Firewood lay stacked in neat rows.

Gram and Abby went through the big double doors of the library. Abby put her books on the counter with a lot of other books. Saturday morning was always busy. People clustered around the front desk to check out. Gram went to look at the cookbooks. Abby headed for the Children's Area.

Abby loved the library. She loved the way the books smelled. She loved the displays with all the new books and the puppets. But most of all, she loved to read. Going to the library was like visiting old friends!

Two boys were smashing toy train engines together in front of the book cart. In the rocking chair, a mom sat reading nursery rhymes to a baby. On the frog floor pillow, two first graders giggled and whispered.

Mrs. Mackenzie perched on her knees by a bookcase. Two stacks of picture books teetered beside her. Behind her, a cart overflowed with even more books. "Hi, Abby!" she said.

"Hi," said Abby. "What a lot of books!"

Mrs. Mackenzie brushed her hair out of her eyes. "I know, isn't it crazy? Last night we couldn't check any books in because of the power failure. Now, I'm way behind putting books away."

"I could help you," Abby offered.

"Would you?" Mrs. Mackenzie asked with a smile. "That would be so nice!"

Abby dropped on her knees. "What can I do?" she asked.

"Do you know how the picture books are shelved?" Mrs. Mackenzie asked.

Abby shook her head. She just knew where to find her favorite books.

"They are filed alphabetically by the author's last name," Mrs. Mackenzie said. She pointed to *The Grouchy Ladybug* by Eric Carle. "See, this book would go under *C* for Carle. Do you see any other books by that same author?"

Abby looked at the books on the cart. She picked up *The Very Hungry Caterpillar* and handed it to Mrs. Mackenzie.

"Thank you so much," Mrs. Mackenzie said. She took a handful of books off the cart and set them on the floor. "Could you help me sort these? Then I'll put them on the shelves."

"Sure," said Abby, her heart beating very fast.

"Just help me for a little while, Abby," Mrs. Mackenzie said. "I want you to have time to choose your own books, too."

"Mrs. Mackenzie?" Abby said softly. "Do you need help very often?"

Mrs. Mackenzie laughed. "I need help every day, Abby. Every night when I go home, there is always something here that I didn't finish."

Abby glanced around to see if anyone else was listening. "I'm asking because our teacher, Mr. Kim, assigned us a project for next month."

Mrs. Mackenzie sat back on her heels. "Can I help you find some books for it?" she asked. "I don't have to file all of these right now. What do you need?"

Abby shook her head. "I don't need books. I need to be a volunteer somewhere. I'm supposed to *help* someone."

Abby took a deep breath. "Mrs. Mackenzie, could I help you?"

The Perfect Job!

For just a moment, Mrs. Mackenzie didn't say anything. Abby held her breath. Then Mrs. Mackenzie smiled. "Abby, I would love to have you help me!" she said. "I am so glad you asked!"

Abby asked again, just to make sure. "Then, I can be your helper?"

"Of course you can!" Mrs. Mackenzie said. "When does your project start?"

"Not until next week," Abby said. "But we have to tell Mr. Kim where we will be working this Monday."

"Do I need to write a letter for you or anything?" Mrs. Mackenzie asked.

"Not until the end," Abby said. "You are supposed to tell whether I did a good job and if I worked all my hours."

"Well, I'll write you a very good letter!" said Mrs. Mackenzie. "Look how helpful you are! You even started early by putting books away today!"

Abby thought of something. "Has anyone else asked to help you?"

Mrs. Mackenzie shook her head. "No one has asked but you, Abby. Do you have friends that need jobs, too?"

"I don't think so," Abby said. "They all found projects before I did."

"Well, I am very glad you asked," Mrs. Mackenzie said. "You can even walk down to the library after school if you like. I could meet you out front."

"That would be fun!" Abby said. Some days her mom let her come to the library after school anyway. Betty always helped her cross the street and the library was right on the other side.

Abby scrambled to her feet. "Would you mind if I go and tell Gram? We have been trying and trying to think of a project!"

Mrs. Mackenzie laughed. "And here I was, wishing I had a helper. Go! Tell her!"

Abby zigzagged around a mom with a stroller and almost collided with an older couple carrying a bag of books. She zipped around the adult book displays, barely missing a man with a cane. She raced down the stacks looking for Gram.

"Slow down," said one of the staff members.

Abby slid into a fast walk. And there was Gram! She was sitting on a stool with a pile of cookbooks beside her. One was open on her lap.

"Gram, guess what!" Abby yelled.

Gram put a finger to her lips. "Not so loud," she whispered.

"Guess what," Abby whispered back.

Gram laughed. "I'll bet they just got a new book that you love!" she guessed.

"No," Abby said. "Guess again!"

"Mrs. Mackenzie's dog had puppies and you want another one like Lucy?" Gram guessed.

"No," Abby said. "I found my project! Mrs. Mackenzie says I can work here at the library!"

Gram pulled her close for a hug. "That's wonderful! All that worrying for nothing! Didn't I tell you that you would find something special?"

This is special, Abby thought. *It's better than visiting the nursing home! It's better than helping Mr. Kim! It's lots better than picking up trash!* Abby twirled around right there in the middle of the library. This was the perfect place to work! She was so happy!

Surprising Mr. Kim

On Monday, Abby ran to school!

Betty started to laugh when Abby reached the crosswalk. "Hey girl, what's up?" she asked.

"I found the best place to do my project!" Abby said. She just couldn't stop smiling this morning.

"Now, what did I tell you?" Betty said, putting her hands on her hips. "I knew something would turn up!" She leaned over. "So, can you tell me or is it a secret?"

Abby glanced around her. There wasn't a third grader in sight. "The library!" she whispered.

Betty's eyebrows popped up like little upside-down smiles. "Are you going to be Mrs. Mackenzie's helper?" she asked.

Abby nodded. "Isn't that the best?"

"It sure is," Betty agreed. "You'll have a lot of fun at the library!"

"I can't wait to tell Mr. Kim!" Abby said, jumping on one leg.

Betty laughed. "Well, go and tell him, then!"

"Bye!" Abby shouted. She turned and ran up the steps to the school.

Most of the students were already in their seats. Abby hung up her jacket in the hall. She carried her book bag to her desk. Sydney waved and Abby waved back.

Abby sat down. Dakota threw a wad of paper. It hit Abby in the back of the head. Abby just looked straight ahead at Mr. Kim.

"Good morning, class," Mr. Kim said. He pointed to a big chart on the bulletin board. "I have everyone's name up here with a space for their Community Helpers job across from it. When I call your name, tell me where you will be working and who will be filling out your report."

Mr. Kim called Sydney's name first. Abby didn't look at her when she answered.

"Katie and I will be visiting Evergreen Nursing Home with Pastor Elizabeth," Sydney said.

"Very good," Mr. Kim said, writing the information in the space on the bulletin board. "Ethan Rossi, what are you doing?"

Ethan looked at his twin sister. "Morgan and I are reading to the preschool class twice a week. Miss Gibson is the teacher."

Abby listened as the kids reported on their projects. When Alexis, Robby, and Noah said they were picking up trash in the park, someone launched a bunch of paper wads from the back of the room.

They plopped down softly around Noah's desk. One landed on Mr. Kim's shoe.

Mr. Kim shook his shoe. The paper skittered across the floor.

"I'm going to pretend that didn't happen," Mr. Kim said. "Clean it up before I turn around." He turned his back to the class and wrote on the chart.

Dakota and Zachary rushed up to pick up the paper. They threw the paper wads in the trash can. Then, the two boys rushed back to their seats as Mr. Kim swung back to face the class.

Mr. Kim looked at Dakota and Zachary. He didn't say anything for a minute. Then, he looked at Abby. "Abby," he said, "what project did you choose?"

The room fell silent. Everyone stared at Abby.

Abby sat up very straight. She smiled at Mr. Kim. "I'm working at the library," she said.

"Here at the school?" Mr. Kim asked as he turned back to the board to fill in Abby's line on the chart.

She shook her head. "No, at Evergreen Library. I'm going to be Mrs. Mackenzie's helper."

"Way to go!" yelled Dakota, drumming his hands on his desk.

Another wad of paper smacked Abby's head. Sydney clapped.

"Well," Mr. Kim said, laughing, "it seems everyone thinks you found a very nice project, Abby! I hope you have fun."

Abby just smiled. She could hardly wait to get started!

Story Time

Gram dropped Abby off at the library on the first day of her project. "I'll do some grocery shopping and come back," Gram said. "Have fun!"

Abby was so excited! Her tummy felt like it had butterflies in it! She was only supposed to work for an hour. She wished it could be longer. She walked through the big double doors.

She heard whistles blowing in the Children's Area. Story Time had just finished. Moms and kids crowded around Mrs. Mackenzie. She was passing out bird whistles. The library sounded like a forest!

A pile of jackets covered the top of a bookshelf. Toys lay all over the floor.

The wooden book cart was almost empty. Most of the books were piled on the rug.

Mrs. Mackenzie bent to zip a little boy's coat. "Abby!" she said. "I am so glad to see you! Can you help me sort out these jackets, please?"

A little girl tugged on Abby's sleeve. "Mine is the pink one!" she said.

Abby looked at the pile of jackets. Six of them were pink! She lifted them down one at a time. "Is this one yours?"

Each time the little girl shook her head. Finally, Abby found a pink jacket with flowers on it. She picked it up.

"That's it!" the little girl said.

Abby helped her put her arms in the sleeves. Then she buttoned the jacket. "Now you are ready to go home!" she said. "My name is Abby. What's your name?"

"Lucy," the little girl said.

Abby laughed. "I have a dog named Lucy! Is your mom here?"

The little girl looked around. "I don't see her."

"I'll wait with you," Abby said. "We can watch for her together."

In just a minute, Lucy's mom came in pushing a stroller. Lucy blew her bird whistle in her baby brother's face.

"Bye, Lucy," Abby said.

"Bye!" Lucy called. Abby could hear her blowing her whistle until the front door shut.

The jacket pile was gone. So were a lot of the kids. Abby stepped back right onto a squeaky toy.

Abby began to pick up the toys. She put them in colored crates. One block tower still stood on the rug. Abby packed the blocks into the red crate. She put the stuffed dinosaurs and dragons in the green one. Trucks and cars went into the blue crate.

When she finished she looked around. The rug looked cleaner. She went to help Mrs. Mackenzie pick up books.

"Thank you for picking up the toys," Mrs. Mackenzie said. "These books just go here in the browser." She pointed at the cart. "They don't have to be in order."

Abby remembered the sturdy board books from when she was little. Her mom had brought dozens of them home to read to her.

Someone called Mrs. Mackenzie to the main desk. Abby scooped up all the board books. She stacked them neatly in the browser. She was all done when Mrs. Mackenzie came back.

"Abby, you are wonderful!" Mrs. Mackenzie said. "I'm so glad I have you to help me!"

Abby smiled. It felt good to help! She was happy to be here.

Mrs. Mackenzie picked up the bag of bird whistles off the bookcase. "Would you like a whistle? I have some left over."

"Sure!" Abby said. "Thank you." She chose a yellow one. She thought she could use it to play with Lucy.

"Could you help carry the puppets back to my desk?" Mrs. Mackenzie asked.

Abby picked up a squirrel and a rabbit. She followed Mrs. Mackenzie to the workroom. Mrs. Mackenzie carried the bear and some books.

The workroom had two desks. On one desk, papers were stacked neatly beside a computer. Mrs. Mackenzie's desk was piled with books, toys, and puppets.

"Where should I put these?" Abby asked.

"Just pile them anywhere," Mrs. Mackenzie said. "I don't have enough space. My desk is always a mess."

Abby put the puppets beside a jar of pirate coins. A gypsy puppet winked at Abby from under a stuffed dragon with two heads. Chocolates spilled out of a painted box with a princess and a frog. Glitter sparkled everywhere. Abby thought Mrs. Mackenzie's desk looked magical.

"Maybe someday you could help me straighten this up," Mrs. Mackenzie said.

Abby looked at all the sparkly books and puppets. "Okay!" she said.

Rubber Frogs and Cow Balloons

A few days later, Abby was walking to the library when Dakota stopped her.

"Wait up!" he yelled.

Abby stopped on the sidewalk outside the library. "What's the matter?" she asked.

"Aren't you going home?" Dakota asked.

"I'm going to the library," she said. "I thought you were helping Mr. Kim."

"I can't," Dakota said. "He has a teachers' meeting."

"Did you miss the bus?" Abby asked.

Dakota kicked a pinecone into the street. "No, my dad is picking me up at four. I thought Mr. Kim needed me today. Can I go to the library with you?"

"Sure," Abby said. She turned and walked toward the big brick building.

"Are you helping Mrs. Mackenzie?" Dakota asked.

Abby nodded. "We're setting up the program room for the movie tomorrow night."

"Cool," Dakota said. "Can I help?"

Abby stopped. "I guess so. You'll have to ask Mrs. Mackenzie. I don't think she'll care."

They found Mrs. Mackenzie by her desk. A pile of puppets and books lay all over the floor.

"What happened?" Abby asked.

Mrs. Mackenzie laughed. "This is called an avalanche. I tried to put one

more book on my desk and everything fell off!"

"Man, what a mess!" said Dakota. He pushed the pile with the toe of his shoe.

Abby giggled. "I'll help you clean it up."

"I'll help, too," Dakota said.

"This is Dakota," Abby said. "He helps Mr. Kim. But Mr. Kim doesn't need him today. Can he help you, too?"

Mrs. Mackenzie laughed again. "I need all the help I can get, Abby!"

Mrs. Mackenzie brought boxes with lids. Dakota put the puppets inside. Abby wrote the names of the puppets on the boxes. They carried them to the storage room. Then, Dakota put them up on the shelves.

Mrs. Mackenzie had stacked up the books on the floor. "These books are for Story Time," she said. "Could you put them on the shelf above my desk?"

Abby stood on a stool. Dakota picked up the books and handed them to her. He found five stretchy rubber frogs and two spotted cow balloons under the books.

"Where do these go?" he asked.

"You and Abby can have them," Mrs. Mackenzie said. "They're left over from Story Time."

"Thanks!" said Dakota. He blew up a balloon and let it go. It zoomed and sputtered around the workroom.

Mrs. Mackenzie put her hands over her head and ducked. Dakota crawled under the desk to get his balloon. He stuffed it in his pocket. He chose three frogs. He put them in his other pocket.

Abby took the other cow balloon and two frogs.

"We need to get ready for Movie Night," Mrs. Mackenzie said. "Can you set up fifty seats? Or are you too tired?"

"We're not tired!" Dakota said.

Mrs. Mackenzie led the way to the meeting room. There, she hooked up the projector and pulled down the screen. Dakota and Abby moved the chairs. They made an aisle down the middle of the room. They put five chairs in each row and five rows on each side of the aisle.

Dakota counted every chair. "That's fifty!" he said.

"Just one more thing," said Mrs. Mackenzie. "Can you tape the extension cord down so no one trips on it?"

Abby cut strips of duct tape. Dakota crawled along the floor taping the cord down. It took fifteen pieces of tape to reach the wall outlet.

"Done!" said Dakota. He flopped down on one of the chairs. "That was a lot of work!"

"Sit down and rest," said Mrs. Mackenzie. "You can watch the previews." She pushed a switch and the screen lit up.

Dakota held his arm out in the aisle and wiggled his fingers. He made a shadow puppet on the screen. Abby sat down next to him. She kept her hands in her lap.

Mrs. Mackenzie brought them lemonade and cookies. "Thank you for all your work!" she said. "This would have taken me a lot longer to do by myself!"

"I like helping at the library," Dakota said to Abby. "Mr. Kim doesn't give me lemonade and cookies. He doesn't give me rubber frogs and balloons, either."

Abby smiled. "Maybe you chose the wrong project," she said.

Lunch with a Vampire

"How's the new job?" Betty asked the next morning. Rain dripped off her duck umbrella. It splashed on her orange poncho and red boots.

"It's fun!" Abby said. "I'm helping with the movie tonight."

"I'm coming!" Betty said.

"We're having cookies and popcorn," Abby told her.

"That sounds yummy," Betty gushed. "Now hurry into school before the rain washes you away, honey!"

Abby splashed up the steps and into the building. Umbrellas stood in puddles in the hall. Jackets dripped on their hooks. Everything felt nasty, damp, and cold. Abby took off her jacket and hung it in the hall.

A paper airplane swooped through the classroom door. Abby ducked. It smashed into the coat rack and crash landed. She bent to pick it up. Dakota ran into the hall with Zachary behind him.

Dakota grabbed the plane and waved it over his head. "I won!" he yelled. "Thanks, Abby!"

Abby followed the boys into the classroom. Sydney and Katie were talking across the aisle. Abby waved but the girls didn't even look up. Katie held up matching blue friendship bracelets. She put one on and gave the other one to Sydney.

Abby slid into her seat and tried to look busy. She tapped her foot against the leg of her desk. *Tap! Tap! Tap!* She waited and waited for Sydney and Katie to stop talking.

Finally, Katie leaned over to get a book out of her backpack. "There is a movie tonight at the library, Sydney," Abby said. "Do you want to go with me?"

Katie straightened up. "Sydney's busy tonight," she snapped. "She's coming to my house for dinner."

Sydney blushed. "Katie's mom invited my family over. I'm sorry, Abby. I can't go to the movie."

Abby turned away so Sydney wouldn't see the tears in her eyes. "It's all right," she said. But it wasn't all right. It seemed as though Sydney and Katie were spending more and more time together. That left no time for Abby to spend with Sydney.

Abby took out her books. She arranged them neatly on her desk. She tried really hard not to look at Sydney and Katie. But all she could hear was Katie talking and giggling.

Dakota zipped up the aisle and landed on Abby's desk. He used two red pencils to drum on her books. "What time should I come tonight?" he asked.

"I have to be at the library at six," Abby said. "But the movie doesn't start until six thirty. I'm only going early so I can help."

"See you at six!" Dakota said. "I want to help, too!"

Mr. Kim walked in. Dakota slid off Abby's desk and shot into his own chair.

Abby turned to look at him. "Don't you have to help Mr. Kim?" she whispered.

"I can do both!" he said.

Abby smiled. At least she would have one friend at the movie tonight.

Katie saved Sydney a seat at lunch. There was no room for Abby at the same table.

Abby ate with Dakota, Zachary, and Ethan. Zachary blew milk out his nose on purpose. Dakota mixed tuna with chocolate pudding and ate it with a plastic knife. Ethan put candy corn on his front teeth and pretended to be a vampire. Then they took turns throwing olives in Zachary's milk.

Abby looked at Katie and Sydney. They had matching pink lunchboxes.

Katie had brought cookies to share. Abby turned away. She took an olive and threw it at Zachary's milk. It plopped right in.

Dakota patted her shoulder. "Good shot!" he said.

Movie Magic

"I hope the rain won't make people stay home tonight," said Mrs. Mackenzie.

"Betty and Gram are coming," Abby said. She stacked the napkins in two neat piles on the refreshment table.

"Is your friend Sydney coming?" Mrs. Mackenzie asked.

Abby shook her head. "She's busy," she said. She didn't want to think about Sydney right now.

"Well, she is going to miss a good movie," Mrs. Mackenzie said. "Maybe she can come next time."

Or maybe not, thought Abby. Maybe Sydney had decided that Katie was her new best friend. Maybe Sydney didn't want to hang out with Abby anymore. She went back to the workroom to get the cookie trays.

Dakota had one cookie in his mouth and another one in his hand.

"Dakota!" Abby said. "Those are for Movie Night! You're not supposed to eat them now!"

"Mrs. Mackenzie said I could try one," he protested. Pink crumbs stuck to his cheek. He smelled like peanut butter and chocolate.

Abby looked at the trays. There were at least five cookies missing. "Why don't you take the lemonade to the program room?" she said. "And don't drink it on the way!"

Abby picked up a cookie tray. She passed Betty on the stairs. Betty was wearing a brown sweatshirt with pumpkins on it.

"Hi, honey!" Betty said. "Mmmm, look at all those cookies!"

"They look really good, don't they?" Abby said.

Mrs. Mackenzie had lined up popcorn bags on the refreshment table. Abby put the cookies beside them.

"Abby," Mrs. Mackenzie whispered, "we need more seats!"

The program room was filling up fast. Two strollers were parked at the back of the room. Most of the chairs were already filled.

Abby could hear a lot of people coming up the stairs. "Dakota and I will get more chairs," she said.

"Make two more rows on each side," Abby told Dakota. "That will make seventy seats."

Dakota looked at the remaining stack of chairs. "What if we run out of chairs?"

"What if we run out of cookies?" Abby asked.

Dakota blushed. "Oops," he said.

Abby picked up a chair.

Someone tapped her shoulder. "Can I help?"

Abby turned around to see Sydney standing there. Her heart started

thumping. "I thought you couldn't come," Abby said. "I thought you were going to Katie's house for dinner."

"I did go for dinner," Sydney said. "But I told my mom that I wanted to come here afterward."

Abby looked around. "Did Katie come, too?"

Sydney shook her head. "I told Katie I wanted to see the movie with you,"

Sydney said. She looked at the floor. "I don't like the way Katie treats you. You're my best friend, Abby."

Dakota took the chair from Abby. "Girls," he muttered and walked off.

"What about Katie?" Abby asked.

Sydney shrugged. "I still have to do my project with her. But, she's not my best friend."

Abby swallowed the lump in her throat. "Thanks," she said.

"Best friends forever?" Sydney asked.

Abby grinned. "Best friends forever!" she replied.

"We need chairs!" Dakota shouted, rushing past them. "Are you two going to help?"

Abby and Sydney started to laugh. "Yes!" they both said.

Technical Trouble

"I think we're ready!" Mrs. Mackenzie called.

The audience quieted down as they waited for the movie to begin. Abby and Dakota breathed a sigh of relief. The popcorn had all been served. The lemonade had been poured. And there were just four cookies left.

Dakota stood by the light switch. Mrs. Mackenzie nodded to him and the lights went off. Mrs. Mackenzie flipped the switch on the projector. Nothing happened. The room stayed dark.

"Wait a minute," Mrs. Mackenzie said. "Turn the lights back on, Dakota."

Dakota switched the lights on. He and Abby ran over to the projector.

"What could be wrong?" Abby asked. "It worked yesterday."

"Maybe something burned out," Dakota said. He looked at the projector. "Nothing happens when you push the power button."

Someone groaned. Everyone loved Mrs. Mackenzie, but she didn't know very much about audiovisual equipment. Last summer the library had shown *Charlotte's Web*. The movie had stopped at the beginning of the last scene. No one got to see the end of the movie.

"Just a minute, everyone," Mrs. Mackenzie said. "I'm sure we can fix this quickly." She was trying to sound cheerful. But Abby could tell she was upset.

Mrs. Mackenzie checked all the wires. Nothing was working. The sound system and the DVD player were off, too.

Dakota dropped to his knees by the projector. One of the men came over to look at it. He took some cords out of the back and plugged them back in again.

Abby bent down to see what Dakota was doing. She noticed the duct tape covering the extension cord had pulled off. She followed the cord to the back of the room. Two strollers were parked on top of it. The cord was stuck in one of the wheels.

"Mrs. Mackenzie?" Abby called, moving a stroller out of the way. "The

extension cord is unplugged!" She carefully untangled the cord from the wheel and plugged it back into the outlet.

Mrs. Mackenzie pushed the switch. The projector's light came on! Happy music filled the room. The audience clapped.

"Thank you, Abby!" Mrs. Mackenzie said.

Abby grinned. "I'll get the lights!" she offered. She ran to turn them off.

Abby and Sydney each got a cookie. They sat in the back of the room with Mrs. Mackenzie. Dakota sat on the floor with a big bag of popcorn.

"I thought we ran out of popcorn," Abby whispered. "Where did you get that?"

"I hid it under the projector table," Dakota said with a grin.

Mrs. Mackenzie sighed. "Well, this was almost a disaster. What would I do without you, Abby?" she said. Then she looked at Dakota and Sydney. "Maybe I need more than just one helper. Maybe I need a whole bunch!"

Abby laughed. "Maybe we could be the Book Bunch!"

Dakota threw some popcorn up in the air and caught it in his mouth. "Hey, that would be cool! Count me in!"

"Me too!" said Sydney, clapping. Sydney's pink and purple friendship bracelet sparkled even in the dark.

Abby smiled. This was the best Movie Night ever!

The Book Bunch!

The next month zoomed by. Abby went to the library on Tuesdays and Thursdays after school. Most days Dakota went with her. Sometimes Sydney went, too. It was fun helping Mrs. Mackenzie. But it was even more fun when her friends helped!

On the last day, Mrs. Mackenzie gave Abby a letter to turn in for her project. Abby handed it to Mr. Kim when she got to school.

Mr. Kim piled all the letters on his desk. He looked at the class. "Well," he said, "you've finished your Community Helpers Projects. Are you glad this assignment is over?"

A chorus of yeses filled the air!

"I don't ever want to pick up trash again!" Noah grumbled.

"Me either!" said Robby. "Ewww!"

Ethan raised his hand. "I sort of liked reading to the preschool kids. Maybe I'll do it again sometime."

"That's great, Ethan. Did anyone else enjoy volunteering?" Mr. Kim asked.

Sydney spoke up. "The people at the nursing home were always happy to see Katie and me. Some of them are really lonely. Maybe our class could make cards for them."

Mr. Kim beamed. "I'm sure we could do that! We can turn it into an art project."

Abby put up her hand. She glanced at Dakota and Sydney. "Some of my friends came to the library with me. We had a lot of fun. We decided to help Mrs.

Mackenzie all the time, even though the project is over."

"That's really nice!" said Mr. Kim. "I'm sure Mrs. Mackenzie is happy to have so many volunteers."

Dakota grinned. "Yeah, we even have a name," he said, drumming on his desk. "We're the Book Bunch! Abby and the Book Bunch!"

Community Service

Would you like to be a community helper, too? You don't have to have a class project to be a community helper. Abby and her friends found lots of places to volunteer and so can you!

- Ask your parents if you can be a volunteer.

- Volunteering is more fun with a friend! See if a friend would like to volunteer with you.

- Look for a job you are interested in. Contact schools, day care centers, nursing homes, animal shelters, libraries, and churches, synagogues, or mosques.

- Agree to a schedule that you are comfortable with. Abby only volunteered two hours a week at her library.

- Volunteering makes you feel good! Have fun!